HEARTS
AND
HOOVES

ORCHARD BOOKS

First published in the US in 2013 by Little, Brown and Company
This edition first published in the UK in 2018 by The Watts Publishing Group

1 3 5 7 9 10 8 6 4 2

A CIP catalogue record for this book is available from the British Library.

ISBN 978 1 40835 237 3

Printed and bound in China

Orchard Books
An imprint of Hachette Children's Group
Part of The Watts Publishing Group Limited
Carmelite House
50 Victoria Embankment
London EC4Y 0DZ

An Hachette UK Company
www.hachette.co.uk

www.hachettechildrens.co.uk

HEARTS AND HOOVES

Adapted by **Jennifer Fox**
Based on the episode "Hearts and Hooves Day"
written by **Meghan McCarthy**

ORCHARD

**Meet the Cutie Mark
Crusaders!**

Apple Bloom

Sweetie
Belle

Scootaloo

Look for these words when you read this book. Can you spot them all?

valentine

smelly

picnic

potion

The Cutie Mark Crusaders
are making a valentine for their
favourite teacher, Miss Cheerilee.

"More lace!" says Sweetie Belle.

"More hoof prints!" says Apple Bloom.

"More glitter!" says Scootaloo.

The ponies celebrate
Hearts and Hooves Day
every year.

They want Miss Cheerilee to have
the best day ever! The ponies give their
teacher the valentine.

"Do you have a special pony
friend?" Sweetie Belle asks
Miss Cheerilee.

"No," Miss Cheerilee says.
That gives the Cutie Mark
Crusaders an idea!

"We will find her a special
pony friend," they say.

They do not have much time.
Hearts and Hooves Day
is almost over.

They have to find the perfect stallion for Miss Cheerilee.
Not too silly.
Not too flashy.
Not too smelly.

"He is the one!" says Scootaloo.

She nods at Big McIntosh.

"My brother?" asks Apple Bloom.

"Big Mac is nice,
and he works hard,"
says Scootaloo.
"They will fall in love,"
says Apple Bloom.

19

The Cutie Mark Crusaders
set up a picnic date for
Big Mac and Miss Cheerilee.
But they do not fall in love.

Later, the ponies see
Twilight Sparkle.
She has a book
about love potions.
It gives them a new idea!

They mix up a love potion
for Big Mac and Miss Cheerilee.

Miss Cheerilee and Big Mac
drink the love potion.

Big Mac and Miss Cheerilee
fall in love right away.
They call each other
silly names like Pony Pie
and Shmoopie Moopie.

"It worked!" the ponies cheer.

But Big Mac and Miss Cheerilee
are TOO much in love.
They stare at each other all day.
They even decide to get married!

Time passes, and the spell is broken!
Miss Cheerilee and Big Mac
are back to normal.
"I hope you have learned something.
Everyone has to find their own special
pony friend," says Miss Cheerilee.